READING ROOM
KARIGON ELEMENTARY
Bkm. SHENENDEHOWA

S0-BAH-396

# THE SPIDER,
# THE CAVE
# AND THE
# POTTERY
# BOWL

OTHER YEARLING BOOKS YOU WILL ENJOY:

MY BROTHER STEVIE, *Eleanor Clymer*
LUKE WAS THERE, *Eleanor Clymer*
SANTIAGO'S SILVER MINE, *Eleanor Clymer*
WE LIVED IN THE ALMONT, *Eleanor Clymer*
THE HORSE IN THE ATTIC, *Eleanor Clymer*
DEAR MR. HENSHAW, *Beverly Cleary*
HENRY HUGGINS, *Beverly Cleary*
COLUMBUS CIRCLE, *Patricia Reilly Giff*
RAT TEETH, *Patricia Reilly Giff*
THE WINTER WORM BUSINESS, *Patricia Reilly Giff*

YEARLING BOOKS/YOUNG YEARLINGS/YEARLING CLASSICS are designed especially to entertain and enlighten young people. Patricia Reilly Giff, consultant to this series, received the bachelor's degree from Marymount College. She holds the master's degree in history from St. John's University, and a Professional Diploma in Reading from Hofstra University. She was a teacher and reading consultant for many years, and is the author of numerous books for young readers.

For a complete listing of all Yearling titles, write to
Dell Readers Service, P.O. Box 1045,
South Holland, IL 60473.

# THE SPIDER, THE CAVE AND THE POTTERY BOWL

*Eleanor Clymer*

*illustrated by Ingrid Fetz*

A Yearling Book

Published by
Dell Publishing
a division of
Bantam Doubleday Dell Publishing Group, Inc.
666 Fifth Avenue
New York, New York 10103

Text copyright © 1971 by Eleanor Clymer
Drawings copyright © 1971 by Ingrid Fetz

All rights reserved. No part of this book may be reproduced or
transmitted in any form or by any means, electronic or
mechanical, including photocopying, recording, or by any
information storage and retrieval system, without the written
permission of the Publisher, except where permitted by law.

The trademark Yearling® is registered in the U.S. Patent and
Trademark Office.

ISBN: 0-440-40166-6

Printed in the United States of America

May 1989

10 9 8 7 6 5 4 3 2 1

CW

For Maeve

# THE SPIDER,
# THE CAVE
# AND THE
# POTTERY
# BOWL

# *one*

IN a certain place in the desert there is a cave, and sometimes outside the cave you can see a spider in its web. And on the shelf in my grandmother's house there is a pottery bowl. All these things are connected, and this is what I am going to tell about. But first I must tell about myself.

I am Indian. My name is an Indian word meaning One Who Dips Water. But in school they call me Kate. In winter I live with my father and mother and brother in a town near the edge of the desert. My father works in a store. There is a garage next to the store and he helps there, too. We have a garden and peach trees. We have a wooden house. We have running water and electricity. We aren't rich, but we have those things.

But in summer I go back to the mesa where my grandmother lives. We used to live there too, but we moved away. Grandmother's house is part of a village built of stone, with many small rooms, all connected, like a wall of houses around an open place. It's a small village. Some of the houses have other houses that were built on top of them when more rooms were needed. The village is very old, many hundreds of years old. When you drive across the desert you can see the mesa, like a high wall of rock ahead of you. And on top is the village.

I love it on the mesa. It is windy, hot in the sun but cool in the shade of the houses, and you can see far out over the desert—the Painted Desert they call it, because it looks as if it were painted. It is beautiful on the mesa, but it is hard to live there. There is no water. The people must carry water up from springs down below. They must carry up everything they need, and they must go down to tend their gardens, and walk a long way through the desert to find grass or plants for their sheep to eat. It is hard work.

That is why some people moved away. My father doesn't mind hard work, but he needed to earn money for us. So we had to go away to the town.

But every summer we come back, my mother and my brother and I. We stay in my grandmother's house. My mother helps Grandmother with the summer work. And I help, too. We go down below and work in the garden, and we dry the corn and squash for the winter. We gather peaches from the orchard at the foot of the mesa, and we dry them. My brother plays with his friends, and rides the burros that live in the corral.

We gather firewood for the stove and for the fireplace, and pile it up for the winter. We plaster the walls to make the house look clean. And we go a few miles away and bring home clay for the pottery.

The pottery is what I love most of all. I love to work the cool wet clay between my hands. When I was little, my grandmother gave me pieces of clay to play with, and I made things out of them. I made little animals: sheep and donkeys and birds.

Then when I got bigger, I watched my grandmother make bowls and jars. She made a flat piece for the bottom. Then she rolled pieces of clay into long rolls between her hands and coiled them on top of the flat piece till she had built up a jar. She smoothed it with a stone or a piece of shell, and shaped it in beautiful curves. When it was dry, she painted it with lovely designs. I watched her hand holding the brush of yucca leaves, slowly painting birds and leaves around the curving sides of the bowl. When she had enough bowls and jars, she built a fire and baked them hard.

People came to buy them, and my father took some to sell in the store where he works. But one bowl was never for sale. It stood on the shelf in the corner. It had been there for as long as I could remember.

The other women in the village made pottery, but I liked the things my grandmother made. There's nothing I wanted more than to make pottery like hers. So I was always happy when summer came and we could go to the mesa.

But this summer was different. My mother did not come. She had to get a job.

For many days I heard my parents talking. There had been no snow during the winter, and all spring it had not rained. The springs did not give much water. The gardens were not growing well.

Where we live, everything depends on water. We

are careful not to waste it. The people plant their gardens with little walls around them to save every drop that might run off. We have dances and prayers and music that help to bring rain. Even our names are like prayers for rain. That is why my name is One Who Dips Water. My brother's name is a word that means Clear Water, but his school name is Johnny.

Anyway, Mother and Father knew they would need money to buy food next winter. There are jobs in summer when the tourists come to stay in the hotels, and my parents decided that my mother should get such a job to earn extra money.

I said, "But what will we do? Won't we go to the mesa? What will Grandmother do?"

Mother said, "Kate, you are big, you will help Grandmother. Johnny will do his share. He is big enough to bring wood and water. Perhaps the neighbors will help with Grandmother's garden. But if the mesa springs are as dry as ours, perhaps there will not be much of a garden. We will need money to help Grandmother, too. When the summer is over and we come to get you, perhaps Grandmother will come with us and live here."

I did not think she would, but I did not say so.

So my father drove us to the mesa in the truck. It is about forty miles. We rode across the desert, between red and black and yellow rocks, and sand dunes covered with sage and yellow-flowered rabbit-brush. I was thinking about the work I would do. I don't mind the work, because it's important. Some day Grandmother's house will be Mother's, and then it will be mine. So I ought to know how to do everything.

A boy doesn't care so much, because the house won't belong to him when he grows up. He has to know about other things. That's why Johnny wasn't so interested in helping. Anyhow, getting wood and water isn't much fun. He wanted to play rodeo. He had a new cowboy hat and a rope for a lasso. And he wanted to go with the big boys and men to herd sheep and work in the cornfields. The little boys like it when the men are willing to take them along. Last year Johnny was too small.

"I hope they take me," he said. "I'm big enough now."

At last we saw the houses and the store and the school at the foot of the mesa. We took the narrow

rocky road up the side of the mesa, and at last we came out in the open space on top.

It was good to be there. We jumped out of the truck and ran to see our friends. My best friend Louisa was there with her mother. She lives on the mesa all the time. I was so glad to see Louisa that we hugged each other. Summer is the only time we can really be together.

My grandmother was waiting for us in the doorway of her house. When I saw her I was surprised.

She looked much older than the last time I had seen her. I had always thought of Grandmother as a strong, plump woman with black hair. This year she looked smaller, thinner, and her hair was gray.

Father noticed, too. He said to her, "Are you all right?"

Grandmother said, "Yes, I am well."

Father carried in the basket of food we had brought, and the boxes with our clothes. He explained why Mother had not come.

Grandmother turned quickly in surprise. But she only said, "Well, if that is the way it is, it will have to be."

I said, "I will help you, Grandmother."

She nodded and said, "Yes, you are a big girl now."

And the neighbors who had come in said, "We will all help."

Father asked about Grandmother's garden. But she said she had not planted a garden this year. Then he asked if she had any pottery for him to take back, and she said, "No, I have not made any."

"Do you need clay?" he asked.

She said, "No, I don't need any clay."

Father said good-bye then. As he was leaving, he said to me, "Remember, if you need Mother or me, go down to the store and telephone, and we will come."

Then he went away, and there we were.

I did not know what to do at first. I thought Grandmother would tell me, but she did not. So I made a fire in the stove and made coffee. We drank some. Johnny went to find his friends.

I said, "Is there something you want me to do?"

Grandmother said, "Later. Now I think I will sleep a little." And she lay down on her bed.

I went outside. It was strange for my Grandmother to be sleeping in the morning. I thought, "Well, after she has a rest, we will do things."

I went to Louisa's house. She was taking care of her baby brother. We played with him and made him laugh. Then Louisa put him to sleep in his cradle, and we went outside.

We talked about school and other things, and then Louisa's mother called out that she needed water. So we got some pails and went to the spring. There is a big spring and a pool at the bottom of

the mesa, and the men bring water up in their trucks, or on the backs of burros. But we went to another spring, a little one, on a path that goes part way down the side of the mesa. The water drips out between the layers of rock, and we hold our pails underneath and fill them.

Later I went back to our house. It was nearly dinner time. Mother had sent some stew, so I warmed it up and cut the bread. Then I called Johnny and we ate.

Grandmother did not eat much. After dinner she went out and sat in the sun.

# two

SO the first days passed. I did everything I could think of. I tried to grind corn on the metate (the grinding stone), thinking it it would please Grandmother. But I did not really know how to do it, and it was easier to cook the ready-made corn meal. I washed the cups and bowls and shook out the bedding. I swept the house.

It did not take long. There are only two rooms. In the main room there is a fireplace in one corner, a table and some chairs, the stove, and Grandmother's bed of rugs and blankets. There are the metates and the pails and jars for water, the shelves for dishes, the yucca brushes for sweeping. (Mother uses a broom, but Grandmother likes the old-

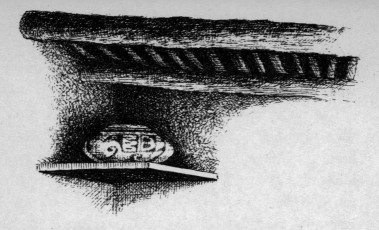

fashioned things.) And in another corner is the small shelf with the pottery bowl.

The other room has two beds, where Johnny and I slept, and the boxes with our clothes.

I would have liked to plaster the walls, but I did not think I could do it myself. Besides I did not want to disturb Grandmother. Sometimes she lay on her bed and seemed to be sleeping. Other times she sat outdoors. But her hands, which used to be so busy, were idle.

Nearly every day some tourists came. In other years, Louisa and I liked to see the tourists. They were so funny. They usually had big cars, and they were afraid of the rough road up the mesa. They went very slowly, hoping they would not meet anybody coming down. When they got to the top, they would get out of their cars and look around. And then they would buy pottery.

But this year I did not like them. I did not like the way they walked around and stared at us and our houses, as if we were something for sightseers to look at. I did not like the way some of the little boys ran after them. Once I saw Johnny and his friends go over to a car and touch it, and Johnny said, "How much did this car cost?" His friend said, "Give us money." I did not like that a bit, and I told the boys to go away.

Then, when the tourists asked for pottery, I had to say that we had none.

My grandmother used to sign her pottery. She would paint the name Anna on the bottom. Her name was Kuka-Am, which means Older Sister, but Anna was easier for white people to say, and they would often come to ask for Anna's pottery. I wondered when we were going to make some, but I did not like to ask.

Then one day I did. There had been lots of tourists, all looking for pottery. When they went away I said, "Grandmother, when will we make some?"

She said, "There is no more clay."

I knew there was none in the storeroom. Always before, there had been chunks of the greyish clay there, waiting to be ground up and soaked in water and shaped into bowls.

Grandmother used to carry it herself from a place she knew, a mile or so from the mesa. Later on Father had brought it in the truck. But this year she had not asked him to get any.

"The bed of clay is used up," she said.

I said, "But there are other beds. Louisa's mother and the other women know where to get clay. I can go with them and get some."

She said, "The clay that I used was very fine. It

needed nothing mixed with it to keep it from crack-ing."

I knew what she meant. Some kinds of clay will crack in the firing unless they are mixed with sand or ground-up bits of old pottery. But the kind she liked was good enough to be used alone. And there was no more of it.

I said, "Well, I will get some other kind, and you can show me what to do."

She nodded and said, "Perhaps. Perhaps later."

I wished my mother were there. I didn't know what to do. Grandmother did not seem to be sick. She just seemed far away.

I said, "Grandmother, shall I send a message to Mother to come? Would you like to see her?"

But she said, "No, let her do her job. That is more important now."

I asked, "When we go home, will you come with us?"

She shook her head and said, "No. My place is here. When I come to the end of my road, let it be here."

So there was nothing to be done, except to do my work and remind Johnny to do his. But most of the time he was nowhere in sight.

Johnny was disappointed too. There were no big boys for him to go herding with, and none of the men wanted to take him to the cornfields. So all he did was play with the burros. When he wasn't doing that, he was drawing pictures in the dust of the plaza with a stick. Sometimes he found a piece of charcoal and drew on flat rocks or anything he could find. Once he drew pictures all over a house wall and got scolded for it.

Anyway, he didn't often bring firewood, so I went for it myself. One day Louisa and I went to get some on the mesa top, beyond the village. We took cloths along, and piled juniper twigs in them. It was hot, there was no shade to protect us from the sun. The wind blew, but that only made it hotter.

I said, "I would like to have a big swimming pool here. I'd jump in and cool off."

Louisa looked at me out of the corners of her eyes. Then she said, "Maybe you wish you were back in the town, so you could go swimming."

I said, "No, I don't. I like it here. Only this summer everything is strange. Grandmother is different."

Louisa said, "My mother says she is getting very

old. She thinks your mother should be here."

I said, "My mother would come if I called her. But Grandmother would not like it."

Louisa was silent for a while. She kept picking up wood and putting it in the cloth. Then she said, "I think it is because Kuka-Am fell. Something happened when she fell."

I said, "She fell? I didn't know that. How did it happen?"

Louisa said, "She went to get water, and when she was bending over, she got dizzy and fell. My mother helped her get home."

I said, "But why didn't she tell us?"

Louisa said, "She said she was well again. Perhaps I should not have told you."

I said, "I am glad you did. Now I understand better."

I did not want to understand, but I did anyway, and I felt afraid. Long ago, there would have been many aunts and cousins to help out. Now there were the neighbors, and me. If I did not send for my mother and anything happened, she would be angry with me. But Grandmother had said no.

We walked back with our firewood. I felt hot and

dusty, and I would have liked to have a bath. Louisa was right in a way. At home, though we had to be careful with water, there was a shower, and there was a swimming pool at the school. But on the mesa there was no water for bathing.

As we came toward the village, there was a loud noise: boys' voices shouting, and burros' hoofs clattering on the stone. Johnny and three other boys had come running into the plaza. They had let the burros out of the corral and were trying to lasso them.

It made a terrible dust, and people began running out of the houses shouting at them.

In the middle of all this there were some tourists in a big white car. The people inside the car looked scared.

Louisa's mother came out with a broom and chased the donkeys away. She told Johnny to go home, and she shouted at the other boys to drive the burros back to the corral.

When things had calmed down, a woman and a

girl got out of the car. There was a man, but he just sat in the car.

The woman and girl stared all around. I suppose I stared at them. The girl was wearing a yellow skirt and white blouse and white sandals. She had long yellow hair. She looked cool, as if she had just had a shower. I guess the car was air-conditioned. She looked at me as if she was sorry for me. Then I remembered that my face was dirty and my hair tangled, and it made me angry. I thought: Maybe she thinks I look like this all the time. I suppose she thinks she's better than me, because she has a big car and nice clothes.

Then I was ashamed of myself for thinking such thoughts.

The woman came over to me and said, "Where does Anna live?"

I said, "Right here." I should have asked what she wanted, but I did not think. The woman started to come in, but Louisa's mother called to her, "Anna is sleeping."

The woman said she wanted pottery. Then I remembered my manners and I said, "Anna is my grandmother. She has no pottery. She has not been

feeling well and hasn't made any."

Louisa's mother said, "There are other women who make pottery." But the woman said, "No, I don't want any other." She peered into the house and saw the bowl on the shelf.

"That's a nice bowl," she said. "Can I buy it?"

At this Grandmother came to the door and said, "No, I can't sell that."

The woman asked, "Why not?"

Then the girl pulled at her mother's arm and said, "Come on, let's go."

Her mother was cross at that and said angrily, "Stop that, Elizabeth." I could see the girl's face get red.

At last they went away. I went in with my firewood and put it down beside the stove. Johnny was sitting at the table.

Then there was a knock at the door. It was one of of the old men of the village.

"Please come in," Grandmother said.

He entered and looked at Johnny. He said, "You and your friends must be more polite. Those strangers are our guests."

Johnny muttered, "They are stupid."

The old man said, "That is not your affair. If you are not careful, the kachinas will whip you."

Kachinas are the spirits that take care of people. They bring rain for the cornfields, and they bring gifts for good children and punishment for bad ones.

Johnny looked frightened.

Grandmother said, "He needs an older brother. In the old days his father or his uncles or brothers would have been here to keep him busy, but now the men are all away."

The old man said, "His father expects him to keep himself busy."

After he went away, I wanted to talk about something else to make Johnny feel better, so I went over to the shelf and lifted the bowl down and held it in my hands.

"Be careful!" said Grandmother.

I said, "That lady wanted to buy Anna's pottery. She didn't know that this isn't Anna's."

Johnny said, "Isn't it? Where did it come from?"

Grandmother said, "It belonged to the Old Ones, our ancestors. Long ago your grandfather was working with some white men in the ruins on the other side of the mesa. He brought it home to me. It was in a cave. There were other bowls, but only this one was perfect. I learned from studying it how to make my own pottery."

Johnny got up and looked into the bowl. There were some smooth stones in it. We both knew what they were. They were Grandmother's polishing stones, the ones she used for rubbing her pottery to make it smooth and shiny. Johnny reached in and took them out and felt them with his fingers.

Grandmother said, "Your grandfather found them in the bowl. A woman used them long ago, and I have used them all these years."

With his finger Johnny traced the design on the bowl. It was a bird with pointed beak and outspread wings.

"It's pretty," he said.

Then he went to put the stones back into the bowl. In doing so, he pushed my arm. The bowl fell to the floor and smashed.

# three

WE both stood there staring at the pieces on the floor. Then we looked at Grandmother. What would she say? I was sure she would be very angry. Maybe the kachinas would whip both of us. After all, I had taken the bowl down, so it was my fault just as much as Johnny's.

But Grandmother did not scold us. She only looked very sad for a moment. Then she said, "Pick up the pieces and put them in a basket. Perhaps we can mend it."

I didn't think we could, but I picked them up and put them with the polishing stones into a basket.

When I looked up, Johnny was gone. I thought,

"I guess he feels pretty bad. I'll leave him alone for a while."

And I began to get supper ready. When it was done, I went out to call Johnny, but he didn't answer. I asked some of the boys if they had seen him, and they said, "Yes, up by the corral." So I went up there, and he was standing patting his favorite burro. She had her nose on his shoulder as if she was sympathizing with him.

I told him to come home and eat, and he said he wasn't hungry; but I said it was time to come anyhow, so he came with me. I had cooked bacon and corn bread, and we had peaches and cake that I had bought at the store. I noticed Johnny ate quite a lot though he had said he wasn't hungry.

After supper Grandmother lay down on her bed, but instead of going to sleep, she began to tell stories.

She told some we had heard before, ones we liked to hear again. There was the story about how our people came here. You see, for a long time they had lived in a land underground. But they did not have enough to eat, so they were looking for a way to get out. And finally they saw a hole in the roof overhead and wondered what was up there. They sent

the hawk up to look, but he could not fly high enough. Then they sent a mockingbird, but he too couldn't fly high enough to see what was beyond the hole. They sent a jay, but he soon came back. In the end they sent the bluebird. He flew away and was gone so long that they thought he must be lost. But at last they heard him singing, and he had come back. He said there was a fine country beyond the hole. So the wise men used their magic to make a ladder high enough to reach the hole, and they all climbed up. And that was how they reached this earth.

She told us why the ants have thin waists. While the people were underground, they stayed in the village of the ants. There was very little food, and the ants were good to the people and gave them most of the food. So as not to feel hungry themselves, they tightened their belts till they were almost cut in half, and this is the way they are to this day.

Then she told about some things that happened while the people were looking for their proper place on this earth. For even after they came through the hole they could not settle down. They had to wander over the earth for many years to find the right place to live. And often there was no water. So their guardian spirit gave them a little clay water jar and said, "One person will be the water carrier. If there is no water, let the water carrier plant this jar in the earth, and as long as you stay there, water will flow from the jar. When you move, you must take it along."

So they did that. "And it has happened," Grandmother said, "that people digging in the ruins, in a desert or on a mountain, have wondered how anyone could have lived there. That's because they didn't know about the magic water jar."

"And then what happened?" Johnny asked.

"They kept on wandering," Grandmother said, "until they came to their proper place, which is here. And so you see, even if things seem hard sometimes, we know it will be all right, because we are in our proper place, the place to which our people were sent."

"Who sent them?" Johnny asked.

Grandmother opened her eyes and looked at him as if she was surprised that he should ask that.

She said, "Maybe it was our Father the Sun, who made the world. Maybe it was the guardian spirit who gave them the magic water jar. But I think it may have been the Spider Woman. She is the Grandmother of us all. She helped the Sun to make animals and plants and people, and she and her twin grandsons keep things in order. If you ask her for help, she will give it to you."

I had heard of the Spider Woman. I knew you must never kill a spider, because it could be our Grandmother Spider herself.

I said, "Can we ask for anything we like?"

Grandmother said, "Yes, but not too much. You must be careful. She is very wise and will know if you are greedy."

Then she told us a story I had never heard before. She said, "On the far side of the mesa, there is a path that leads to the fields below. And beside the path there is a spring. It is not the spring we all use. It is a very small secret spring. There is a hollow place near by, under the rocks. That is where Grandmother Spider lives. It is her secret house. If you see her there, spinning her web, you must not stop. You must lay a stick of firewood beside the path for the Spider Woman, and hurry on. If you stop to talk to her, she may invite you into her house. You may see her twin grandsons, and they may try to get you to come in. Once you go in, you may have to stay there. So be careful, and do not go that way."

Then she closed her eyes and I could tell from her breathing that she was asleep. Johnny was almost asleep. I pulled him up and led him over to his bed and he fell on it, and was sound asleep in a minute.

Then I went to bed myself. I thought about the stories. Why did Grandmother tell us those stories? Especially the one about the spring. Which spring was it? Could it be the one where Louisa and I sometimes went for water? No, it couldn't be. It must be one somewhere else.

I had a strange dream. I dreamed that out of the fireplace came something small and gray. It was a spider. It looked all around and waved its little feet in the air as if it was looking for something. It ran up the wall to the shelf. I looked, and there was the brown pottery bowl where it had always been. I thought: Oh, I'm so glad it wasn't broken after all. The spider ran inside the bowl and disappeared, and then I woke up and it was daylight.

Sometimes dreams fade away as soon as you wake up, but this dream was as clear as if it had been real life. The first thing I did was to jump out of bed to look at the shelf, to see if the bowl was there, but of course it wasn't.

Then I saw something else. Johnny wasn't there. I thought it was strange that he should be out so early. Most days it was hard to get him out of bed. I looked outside the door but he was not in sight. I wondered if he had gone for water, but the pails were empty. So I put my clothes on and went myself.

It is lovely on the mesa early in the morning. The air is cool and fresh. The sun was coming up and it made the houses look as if they were painted with light red paint. Far below, the desert was painted too, pink and red and gray. The moon was still in the sky. I was glad to be alone out there. I got the water and started back.

At the top of the path I met a couple of men who were going to work in their fields. I could tell because they had their hoes.

One of them was angry. He was saying, "I don't see how she could have gotten out."

I said, "Good morning, did you lose something?"

He said, "Yes, my burro. She got out of the corral somehow. I don't know how because the others aren't

out. Did you see her?"

I said, "No, but I'll look for her." I hurried home. Grandmother was awake. I said, "Did you see Johnny?"

She hadn't seen him. I was sure he had something to do with the burro. It was the one he liked so much.

I thought: He must be afraid he will get a bad whipping. I knew the old man had talked about the kachinas the day before just to frighten him a little. I did not think he would really be punished much. But since he had not only taken the burros out but broken a piece of pottery, maybe he thought he had been very bad, and so he had run away.

I said to Grandmother, "One of the neighbors' burros is missing. Maybe Johnny has taken it, not knowing the man wanted it for work this morning. I will go and see if I can find him."

Grandmother nodded and said, "He is troubled about the bowl. Tell him it does not matter. I am not angry. Last night I was sad, but now I think that perhaps it had to be. The Old Ones may have wanted it back."

I was just going out when she said, "Wait. Eat first. And take some food with you."

So I ate some bread and cold bacon and drank some coffee, and then I wrapped some food in a cloth and put it in a basket. Then Grandmother said, "Wait," again. "Take a bottle of water."

I said, "But I'm coming right back."

She said, "You do not know. If he took the burro, you may have to go a long way. It is good to be prepared."

So I started. First I went to the corral. It was true that the little female burro was gone. But which way did she go? I looked around on the ground and found some little hoofmarks. Then I looked to see which way they went.

Back of the village, the mesa top stretches out like a huge table. That is why it is called a mesa. It means table in Spanish, and when the Spaniards came, they made the Indians use Spanish names for things. Only we use our own names too, for things that are important.

Well, this mesa stretches for miles. Desert plants grow on it, juniper and sagebrush, and some cactus. I started to walk away from the village, and I could see where twigs and leaves had been broken, and I thought that must be the way Johnny went.

I found a path where sheep had run. There were no sheep then, but sometimes the men take the sheep there when it has rained and there is fresh green stuff for them to eat. And in the path were some little hoof-prints. I followed them as fast as I could. I wondered why Johnny had gone that way. If he was going to run away, why hadn't he gone down to the road and tried to get home to Mother and Father?

Then I remembered Grandmother's stories, especially the one about the Spider Woman and the spring, and I wondered if Johnny wanted to find the Spider Woman's house and go inside and escape. Perhaps he thought she would be kinder to him than the people in the village.

I wondered if the story could be true. When you go to school in town you learn different things from what you learn on the mesa, and you wonder if the old stories can be true. But when you get back to the mesa, they have meaning for you, and you feel they are true.

The mesa has valleys in it, like big cracks in the table top. Some of those valleys are wide and have good soil for planting corn. We call them washes, because when there is a thunderstorm the water washes down them like a flood. The men put little fences of branches and twigs around their plants to protect them, so they won't be all washed away. If there is a big storm, though, some of the crops do get washed away.

I looked up at the sky and thought: I'm glad it's not going to rain today—though we had all been praying for rain for many days because it was so dry. But there were only white clouds in the blue sky, the fluffy kind that never do anything.

I was coming to one of those washes. The path led down the slope to the cornfields at the bottom. I was getting very hot and thirsty. The sun beat down on my head and I wished I had a hat. I took the cloth that was around the food and tied it over my head. Then I took a drink of water. I was glad I had it.

Then I was ready to start down into the valley. It wasn't steep like the edge of the mesa where the village is, still it was pretty far down. I thought: How do I know Johnny is down there? I wished for one of those glasses that the tourists carry around their necks. I squinted my eyes, and yes, down in the valley I saw a boy on a burro. They looked very tiny. I yelled, "Johnny!" But of course he couldn't

hear. So I started down. The ground had a lot of loose sand and stones, and I slid part way down, holding on to bushes as I went. At last I got to the bottom and then I had to walk around a cornfield. I noticed that the corn looked thin. There hadn't been enough water. Farther down the wash were some more fields. I saw men working in them, bent over and digging.

I was getting tired and I thought: Why am I hurrying? Johnny knows the way back, and besides he has the burro.

But then I looked up at the sky and I saw that there was good reason to hurry. Instead of the fluffy white clouds, all of a sudden there were thunderclouds, tall gray clouds standing like mountains in the west. The sun was still bright, and as long as the clouds did not cover the sun I did not feel frightened. But they were moving. In the desert a storm can come up in a few minutes. I began to run and to shout, "Johnny!"

He heard me and stopped, and then turned the burro and came toward me. I ran as hard as I could and pointed to the sky, and he understood. At last I came up with him. I was out of breath and couldn't talk, but I climbed on the burro and beat her with my heels to make her run. We were in the middle of the valley and it was maybe half a mile to the opposite side, to a higher spot where we would be safe. Just in time we got there.

In a few minutes we heard thunder. Then the cloudburst came. The rain poured down and in no time the wash was running like a river. We would never have been able to get out if the water had caught us.

Mud and rocks and tree branches came tumbling down in the roaring water. The rain poured on us. I thought: Yesterday I wanted a shower. Now I'm getting it, and my clothes are getting washed, too.

I looked down at the cornfields. The men were running up the bank to get away from the flood. I hoped the corn was not all washed away. I looked to see what Johnny was doing, but he was not beside me, only the burro with ears hanging down and the rain dripping off her.

Then I heard Johnny yell, "Come up here!"

He had found a cave, really an overhanging arch in the rock, and was standing there out of the rain. I pulled the burro and went up there too, and we

sat down and watched the rain fall. We sat for a long time. I squeezed the water out of my hair and skirt, and we ate the food I had brought. Johnny was very hungry. He hadn't thought about taking food with him.

I asked, "Where were you going?"

But he wouldn't tell. I said, "Maybe you were going to look for Grandmother Spider."

Then he laughed and said, "No."

I said, "Well, then what? Did you think you'd find a magic water jar?"

He said, "If I tell you, you'll laugh at me."

I promised not to laugh. Then he said, "Grandfather found that bowl in the ruins where the Old Ones used to live. I broke it, so I was going to find another."

I said, "But Johnny, there aren't any left. The white people took them all away long ago."

He said, "White people are stupid. They couldn't find them all. I would find one that they didn't see."

I said, "But where are you going to look? I don't see any ruins around here."

He said, "Grandmother said they were on the other side of the mesa."

I said, "I think she meant a place far from here."

We stood up and looked around at the rock shelter we were in. It might have been a good place for the Old Ones to live, though if their houses had ever been there, they had crumbled away. But at the back, under one end of the arch, there was a crack, really a hole in the rock, partly filled with stones and sand, and we noticed that a trickle of water ran out of it and down the slope.

"There must be a spring in there," I said.

"Let's go in," Johnny said. "It looks like a deep hole. Maybe there are some ruins inside."

I said, "There could not be ruins in there."

"Well, I'm going," he said, and he got down on his hands and knees and started to crawl in.

Just then I noticed something. Near the entrance, a spider web was stretched across the branches of a little bush. I would not have seen it if the sun hadn't come out, and drops of water on the threads sparkled in the light. In the middle of the web was the spider with her legs spread out. Some little flies were buzzing about. One of them hit the web and was trapped. At once the spider pulled in all her legs and jumped on the fly. I thought how clever she was to make her web by the spring where the flies would come.

Then I thought, "Maybe it's the Spider Woman!" And I shouted to Johnny, "Don't go in!" But it was too late. He was inside the hole. Now, I thought, the Spider Woman will get him and he will have to stay in her house forever.

I felt frightened. But I could not let him go in there alone. I tied the burro to a bush and crawled in after Johnny.

It was pretty dark inside. At first I couldn't see anything. Then my eyes got used to the darkness, and I saw Johnny at the back of the cave. The cave was larger inside than I had thought it would be. Its floor was damp with the water that trickled down from the wall. I guess the water flowing for many years had hollowed out the cave.

"Did you find anything?" I asked.

"Yes," said Johnny. "An old basket, and a stick."

I went over to look. Somebody had been digging there, and had gone away and left the things behind. I tried to lift the basket but it was heavy. I dragged it to the entrance and looked inside.

Johnny said, "It's just a lot of dirt. I wanted to find pottery."

I said, "Johnny, you did!"

He thought I was joking. He said, "It's only sand."

I said, "It's not sand. It's clay. There's clay in this cave. We can make pottery with it."

# *four*

SO I got my basket, and Johnny took off his shirt. The clay was between two layers of rock in the wall at the back of the cave. We took the old digging stick and dug it out. We put it in Johnny's shirt to carry it. We wanted to take the clay we had found in the old basket but it was heavy, and besides the basket was rotted with dampness, and I was afraid it would break, so we left it there. I wondered who the woman was who had been digging and why she had gone away and left her things behind.

We took as much clay as we could carry and went outside. The sky was blue. The water was still running down the wash, but we could cross it. We loaded our clay on the burro and started home.

Johnny led the burro down the slope, but I stayed behind. I went back to the place where the spider web hung. The spider had sucked the juice out of the fly and was waiting for another.

I bent down and said, "Thank you, Grandmother Spider. I saw you last night in my dream. I thought you were telling me something. Now I think I understand." Then I looked around for a piece of firewood to lay beside the spring. I couldn't find one so I laid down the digging stick that I had in my hand.

Maybe this wasn't really Grandmother Spider's house. But it seemed like a good place for it. It was so quiet! The land was so big and so empty. There was no one there but me, and farther down the slope, Johnny and the little burro. I almost expected to see the Spider Woman's twin grandsons standing in the path in front of me. But there was no one. I ran to catch up with Johnny, and we led the burro down the slope, then past the cornfields. Some of the fences had held but others had been washed away by the storm, and some of the corn plants were torn up and drowned.

We climbed the other side of the wash and walked

across the mesa to the village. It was getting toward evening. We had been gone a long time. I began to think that Grandmother must be wondering where we were. But I didn't expect what happened.

When we got to the village, the neighbors ran out to meet us looking very upset. Louisa came and hugged me, and her mother took hold of Johnny and said, "Are you all right? Nothing happened to you?"

I couldn't understand her. I said, "Why should anything happen?"

She said, "One of the big boys just came home and said there was a terrible flood. Then Louisa said she had not seen you all day, and your grandmother said you had gone somewhere. We thought you must be drowned. We were just going to look for you."

I said that we were not drowned, that we had climbed up away from the flood and waited till it was over. She scolded us and said, "Never go away without telling me. What if something had happened to you! What would I tell your parents?"

She wanted to know why Johnny wasn't wearing his shirt, and I said we had a present for Grandmother wrapped in it. Then we went into our house.

Grandmother was sitting inside the door waiting for us. She looked sad and small and very old.

I said, "Here we are."

She said, "So you found him. Where did you go?"

I wanted to say, "To Grandmother Spider's house." But I was afraid she would think I was joking. You must not joke about such things. So I just said, "Across the wash, and we have brought you a present from there."

I laid Johnny's shirt on the floor and untied it. She bent down and took a handful and felt it with her fingers.

"Clay!" she said. "The best kind of clay!" She smiled at me. "Where did you get it?"

I told her, "Across the wash there is a kind of cave, really just a hole in the rocks with water trickling from it. We found a basket of clay and a digging stick."

Grandmother said, "I know that place. A woman was digging there. She had her child with her, and the child was playing outside. There was a storm, and she ran out to save the child and never went back."

I asked, "Did she save the child?"

She said, "Yes, the child is grown up now. But we never went back there. We thought it was bad luck. But you see after many years it is time for good things to happen. It doesn't hurt to wait." Then she looked at Johnny and asked, "Why did you run away? And why did you take the burro?"

He looked a little scared, because he knew he shouldn't have taken the burro without permission. But he was brave.

He said, "I was sorry I broke the bowl. I wanted to find another bowl in the place where the Old Ones lived. But I didn't know how far it would be so I took the burro. It's a good thing Kate came too because I forgot to take food."

Grandmother said, "You'll remember next time. Never go out into the desert without food and water. You might have had to stay all night."

Johnny said, "But I didn't find a bowl. Kate says there are no more left. She says the white people took them all away."

Grandmother said, "They could not take them all. There are still many left, but they are buried in the earth. You would have to dig deep to find them. But what you did find is better. We will make our own bowls now."

Then she said to me, "Now we will eat, and then we will take care of the clay."

So I put food on the table and we ate, but we were so tired that we did not do anything more till the next morning. Then Grandmother told me what to do, and watched while I did it.

I broke up the clay into lumps and ground up the lumps on the metate till it was as fine as cornmeal. I sifted out all the pebbles that were mixed in it. I wet the clay in a pail and put wet cloths over it to keep it soft.

Then I started to make a bowl. I took some clay and made a flat pancake for the bottom, using an old plate to hold it steady. I took more clay and rolled it between my hands into a long roll. I laid it along the edge of the pancake and pinched it in place.

Then I added more and more rolls till the sides of the bowl were built up. I kept wetting my hands in a pail of water and smoothing the clay. Now and then Grandmother took the bowl and fixed it where I had made it too thick or too thin. Her hands had made so many pots that they knew just what to do.

Johnny sat watching us and drawing lines in the dust with a stick to amuse himself.

When the sides of the bowl were high enough, Grandmother took some dried pieces of gourd shell out of a basket. They were what she used for shaping the bowl. She took a piece that was curved just right and held it against the side of the bowl and pushed from inside, till it was shaped like the curve of the gourd. Then she let me do it.

When the bowl was finished, we set it in the shade to dry, not in the sun, for then it would dry too fast and crack.

I was tired. It had taken me a long time. I began to think about cooking dinner. I went into the house. The water pails were full, and there was a pile of juniper twigs for the fire. Johnny had done it when I wasn't looking.

We only made one bowl. We did not have enough clay for any more. When it was dry, it was time to put on the slip. Slip is a coating of very fine white clay. Grandmother had some in her storeroom. We made a thin paste and rubbed it on with a rag. When that was dry, the next thing was the polishing.

Grandmother gave me her polishing stones and said, "They will be yours." And I polished the bowl till it was as shiny as glass.

Then we had to paint it. Grandmother sent me to the storeroom for her pot of black paint. She had made it the year before. She had gathered tansy mustard and boiled it with water till the water was all boiled away and just a black paste was left. Now it was hard and dry. We pounded it into powder and mixed it with water. Then Grandmother took the bowl, and her brush of yucca leaves, and began to paint. She painted a line all around the top with one gap in it, to keep off bad luck.

Then she gave the brush to me, to paint the design. But I had never painted, and I was afraid to spoil the bowl. I sat with the brush in my hand, wondering how to start.

Then Johnny came up behind me. He said, "Let me do it."

I said, "Do you know how?"

He took a piece of charcoal from the stove and drew a design on the wall. It was what he had been drawing in the dust, and it was the design that had been on the broken bowl, a bird with a sharp beak and strong curving wings. I gave him the brush, and he painted it around the bowl.

Grandmother watched him and said, "It is very good."

Then it was time to bake the bowl. But we didn't want to make a fire for just one bowl. We asked the neighbors if anybody wanted to bake pottery. Soon we had about a dozen pieces. Louisa's mother helped us make the fire.

It had to be made just right, with stones to set the pots on, and wood underneath and sheep dung on top. It had to be sheltered from the wind, or the pots would be smudged. When all was ready, Grandmother sprinkled cornmeal and said a prayer. Then she lit the fire.

It was a long time before the fire died down and the bowls were cool enough to touch. When we took them out, our bowl was perfect, with not a single crack. Grandmother looked at it a long time.

Then she said, "Children, it is good. Now we will ask your mother to come."

I said, "Grandmother, but you are all right again!"

She said, "You are right. I was sick before, but I

did not want your mother to know. She had to do her job, and it would have made her too sad. But now I think we will tell her. And maybe she will want to come home and help us make pottery. Maybe we can earn money that way, so she will not have to work in the hotel."

So Mother came and stayed the rest of the summer. She went with us to get clay. She taught me the right words to say when I was digging, because when you take something from the earth you should ask permission and give thanks.

We made pottery the rest of that summer. Johnny

helped us with the designs. My mother is a good potter, almost as good as Kuka-Am. Grandmother didn't make much of the pottery, mostly she did the polishing. It was easier for her. But she signed some of the pieces, because it pleased the tourists. Father took some to sell in the store where he works, and when people heard that they could get Anna's pottery, they started coming to buy it.

One day a car came up the road to the village. It was a big white car, and it stopped and a woman and a girl got out. I went out to meet them, and the girl remembered me. I remembered her, too.

I said, "Hi, you came back."

She said, "Yes. We went all the way to California, and now we're going home, but I wanted to come here on the way. My mother and father didn't want to come, but I made them."

I asked her, "Where do you live?"

She said, "We used to live in Chicago but now we're going to live in New York. We have to move a lot on account of my father's job. I wish I could stay here."

I said, "Maybe you wouldn't like it here."

She said, "Yes, I would. It's so old. It's as if this place has been here forever. You'd always know where you belonged."

Her mother called to her to hurry up, and she went. I remembered that I envied her once. I didn't envy her any more.

I remember that she looked at the bowl on the shelf, the one Johnny painted, as if she would have liked to have it. We still keep it there, and Grandmother keeps her polishing stones in it.

Grandmother is still living in her house. It was her mother's mother's, and some day it will be mine. I'll go away, but I'll always come back, I think. And whatever happens, I'll always keep that bowl.